What Happens When Good Food . . .
Goes BAD.

Written by Justine Fontes
Illustrated by MADA Design

Meredith® Books
Des Moines, Iowa

See the Ike on the cereal box? That's me, Dex Dogtective, product icon, or Ike, for Cinnamon Sleuth Cereal. By day this supermarket is a great place to buy groceries . . .

Look for:

hair gel

potato chips

raisins

Cheazel the Weasel

magnifying glasses

ice cream bars

Lord Flushington

MARKETROPOLIS

. . . but at night it becomes the Marketropolis! Here Ikes can be sweet or sour, but when good food's gone bad, we have the U.S.D.A. or the United Supermarket Defense Association, which I run.

Look for:

Polar Penguin

milk

Fat Cat Burglar

cereal

Hairless Hamsters

price tag gun

Cheazel the Weasel

My best friend, Daredevil Dan, usually helps me out of sticky situations, or I should say he tries. Someday Dan's going to make that loop-da-loop—instead of crashing!

Look for:

toilet bowl cleaner

Dr. Si Nustrix

Cheazel the Weasel

violin

raisins

Vlad Chocul

ice bucket

Sunshine went to look for Dan after his crash—now she's gone too! I searched every aisle, but I can't find her. So I quit running the U.S.D.A. and went to the CopaBanana.

Look for:

Tiki Taki

Cheazel the Weasel

bowls of chips

raisins

Hairy Hold

toothbrush

chocolate bars

One night, Lady X, the new Brand X Detergent Ike, struts into the CopaBanana. A few minutes later she starts a fight between the sweet and salty snacks.

Look for:

Twinkleton

Captain Krispy

pineapples

seltzer bottles

Cheazel the Weasel

Lola Frutola

Polar Penguin

bowl of potato chips

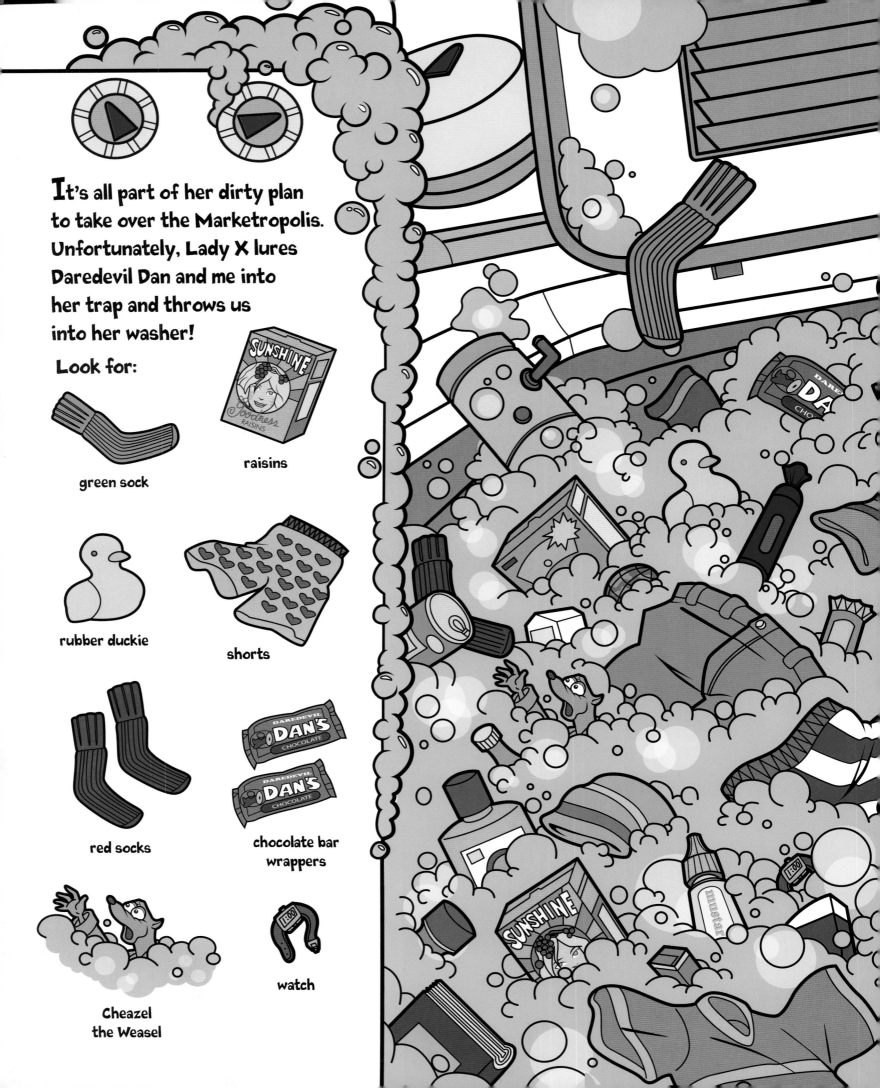

It's all part of her dirty plan to take over the Marketropolis. Unfortunately, Lady X lures Daredevil Dan and me into her trap and throws us into her washer!

Look for:

green sock

raisins

rubber duckie

shorts

red socks

chocolate bar wrappers

Cheazel the Weasel

watch

Luckily, we escape and discover that Brand X has a much more sinister plan! Brand X wants to take over all of the Marketropolis.

Look for:

Won Ton

Francois Fromage

cereal

chocolate bar wrappers

hair gel

Cheazel the Weasel

X-O-Bytes

After I lost Sunshine, I didn't want to get involved anymore. But I have to do the right thing, even if I'm scared. And I know that when we Ikes all work together . . .

Look for:

BRAND
X
WITH ELIXER
Mashed Potatoes

mashed potatoes

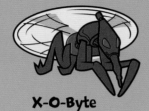

X-O-Byte

Brand X
soldiers

toast

Cheazel
the Weasel

WHIPP
CREF

whipped cream
cannon

lumberjack

PEAS

Brand X soldier

... there's no stopping us! At my signal Lord Flushington activates the sprinklers to wash away Brand X's dreams of taking over the world.

Look for:

Sunshine

Twinkleton

bowl cleaner

X-O-Bytes

trash bags

Cheazel the Weasel

Brand X Ike

The only way to save Sunshine is the loop-da-loop. "Dan, the secret's inside! Just believe in yourself!" I shout. Dan does, and it's a happily-ever-after for us all!

Look for:

Cheazel the Weasel

Captain Krispy

cereal

Lord Flushington

frosted donut

chocolate bar wrappers

X-O-Byte